Deadly Don's Suprise Baby

An Age Gap Mafia Romance

Piper Raven

Copyright © 2023 by Piper Raven

All rights reserved.

No portion of this book may be reproduced in any form without written permission from the publisher or author, except as permitted by U.S. copyright law.

Contents

Introduction	IV
1. Dante	1
2. Sofia	8
3. Dante	14
4. Sofia	21
5. Dante	27
6. Sofia	33
7. Dante	38
Deadly Don's Secret Baby Sneak Peek	45

Introduction

I cashed my v-card in for a sizzling one-night stand that's left me with a baby bump.

This wasn't supposed to happen. Being captive to my crime family, the only value I possess is my v-card.

On my first night of freedom, beyond my family's protection, I'm thrust into ecstasy by a nightclub owner.

Dante's an older, dark haired stallion that's cocky and confident. Needless to say, it was the best night of sin I've ever had.

Now, a year later, my heartless father sells me to a rival crime family...the Vietti's. To him it's business as usual.

The Vietti men are brutal alpha males I've been raised to hate. Now I'm their hostage.

What's worse, they think I'm still chaste. And with a baby growing inside me and no v-card, I'm worthless.

I've traded one hell for an even greater one... And my fate hangs on a knife's edge.

Chapter 1

Dante

The hounds of Hell are out tonight!

Saturday night and it's *my* nightclub that's got all the hottest pieces of ass on the dance floor.

As usual.

It's well-known that my club is the place to be on a night like tonight. Ladies get in free while gentlemen pay a hefty fee. Three women to every man means no one is having a dull night.

"Lemon drop martini, Boss?"

With a nod, I take the drink the bartender's made then take a sip while scanning the gyrating crowd — looking for my next victim.

And there she is.

Dark hair, the color of sin and seduction, it hangs all the way to her narrow waist like a sheet of satin. Alabaster skin makes her glow under the flashing lights.

Moving smoothly in her direction, I end up right behind her as she shakes her voluptuous ass. One of her girlfriends jerks her head, gesturing to me as I dance behind her. She turns to look at me with wide eyes as blue as a summer sky. "Hi."

Saying nothing, I nod, moving in close enough so our bodies graze the tiniest bit. Offering her my drink, I find it cute when she shakes her head. "I don't drink from strangers."

Finding her choice of words funny, I can't help the chuckle that comes out of my mouth. "You can drink from me any time you'd like. I happen to taste delicious."

Her alabaster skin flushes red in an instant, her head drops, and she tries to disappear into the crowd. I'm not going to allow any of that nonsense, though.

With a swift move, I take her into my arms while delivering my now empty glass to a passing waitress before dancing away with her. She and I are complete opposites, and as they say, opposites attract. Our age gap is the only gap between us as I pull her close.

"Um, my, uh, friends."

"I don't want to dance with them. I want to dance with *you*." Swirling her around, her feet leave the floor as squeals of laughter flow from her. It's the best sound I've heard in a very long time.

"I've never danced before." Gripping my shoulder with her small hand, she tries to hold on as I move faster.

"Funny, you're doing a bang-up job of it for a novice." Pulling her close, our bodies move like one, leaving flames in our wake — the heat between us is undeniable.

"I mean, with a stranger. I haven't danced with anyone but family before." Biting her lower lip, she forces the blood from it, leaving it pale.

My mouth waters, wanting to bite that lip until it bleeds. "Dancing is just like sex, you know." Grinding my cock against her, it's steadily rising with desire for her. "You shouldn't do it with family. It's much better with a stranger."

The poor thing blushes fiercely, ducking her head. "You're a bad boy, aren't you?"

"I am anything but that. I am a *man*, through and through." Slowing our movements, I hold her close, inhaling her sweet scent. "Jasmine and vanilla."

Her blue eyes meet mine, intrigue filling them as they sparkle in the flashing lights. "How'd you know that?"

"It's a gift." Leaning in, I sniff the small spot behind her ear, knowing it tickles her in the best way. "I've got lots of gifts I'd love to share with you."

"What kind?" she asks with such innocence that I'm unsure how to take it.

It could very well be sarcasm, but she's not using the right tone for that. Finally, I just ask, "What kind of gifts could I share with you? Is that what you're asking?"

"Yes." With her wide smile and eyes bright and full of wonder, she's the most adorable woman I've ever seen.

So this should shock her in ways she's never been shocked before. "The gift I was talking about is my cock. Or *you* might call it my manhood or even the more pedestrian word, penis."

I cannot help but adore the way she ducks her head then buries her face in my shoulder. The heat from her embarrassment flows through her entire body. Just as I think I've broken her, embarrassing the sweet thing too much, she raises her head and looks me dead in the eyes. "What else?"

Laughing, I can't imagine what else she could possibly mean. "My huge cock isn't enough for you?"

"You said gifts, plural. Not just one gift. So your giant cock is one gift. What other gifts would you like to share with me?"

And here I thought I had a shy little thing in my arms. But how wrong I have been. "I would share my unique abilities to wield my enormous cock as if it were a magic, manly sword that only wants to penetrate your deepest, darkest... wettest recesses."

Arched brows, her expression on the stoic side, I find her utterly captivating. "You mean my vagina?"

"I like to call it a cunt." I watch her face contort with the word I knew would set her off. "You have a problem with me calling your vagina a cunt?"

"Call it whatever you want." Her red lips quirk to one side playfully. "It's not like you're going to get anywhere near it."

Grinding my erection against her hot sex, I smile. "Oh, but I'm already extremely near it. Only your thin dress is between us. One layer of fabric is all that separates us."

"And my panties. Let's not forget those."

"Unless they're made of metal and adorned with a padlock, those too can be ripped away from your body in the blink of an eye." It has been a very long time since any woman has taken my mind off business entirely. I'm not sure that's a good thing.

Looking around, I scan the packed room, finding nothing out of the ordinary. It's not like I have the privilege of completely letting my guard down — ever.

When my eyes come back to hers, I see something different in them. "You are, um, well, very graphic."

"Have I offended you?" I almost hope I have.

With a shake of her head, she smiles again. "I've heard a lot of things in my life, even with being sheltered."

"If you've lived such a sheltered life, what are you doing here, in a nightclub?"

"This is my first time out like this."

"Your first time at a nightclub?"

"Yeah." Dipping her head, she seems a little embarrassed.

And that's a bit worrisome. "You are old enough to be in here, aren't you?"

"I'm twenty-two. This just hasn't been allowed before. But tonight's a celebration. For all I know, it might never happen again. I'm lucky I got to come out this time."

"What has you celebrating?" The music changes to something fast, but I don't want to let go of her yet. So I hold on to her, trying to dance our way out of the enthusiastic crowd.

"I graduated with my bachelor's degree, majoring in accounting."

"That's cool. Are you going to do something else to celebrate? That's quite an accomplishment, and I would think you might do a lot more than just go out to some club as your reward." I watch her face fall, as if I have reminded her of something unpleasant. "Or did you already do something else, and this is the last thing you're doing before getting back to the day-to-day grind?"

"No, this is it. This is all I get to do. Tomorrow, I begin working." Her eyes cloud over. I realize how much I hate to see her like this.

Why I care is beyond me. It's not like me to get involved with anyone, let alone some girl I just met. "Where are you going to work? Maybe I'll stop by. You know, make sure your pretty face has a smile on it."

"You can't come see me at work. I'm going to be working from home."

"So you don't want me to come to your home?"

"I can't have people over. The idea you had, the one about me doing more to celebrate my achievement, it made me think. I've always wanted to see the world. You know, just travel and see things."

"I could show you the world, baby." Easing my grip on her, I move to take her hand in mine, to lead her off the dance floor so we can go somewhere and talk — among other things.

There's just something about this girl. Sweet, innocent, and sad too. Something inside me wants to take away all that sadness.

With her behind me, I lead her through the throng of people but feel her hand slip out of mine. Turning around to grab her hand again, I don't see her. "Hey!"

Scanning the entire place, I don't see her anywhere. "You've got to be shitting me. That little shit ditched my ass!"

Can't say I saw that coming. Son of a bitch!

Chapter 2

Sofia

He's trying to seduce me!

Escape is all I can think about. The man, tall, muscular, and the most handsome thing I have ever seen in real life, is trying to seduce me. He wants nothing more than sex from me.

Just like my father said all men would want.

I had no idea he was so right. And I hate the fact that I thought differently too. In my mind, men were gentle souls who were merely misunderstood.

Boy, was I wrong.

My one night out and I have already ruined it. Darting into the ladies' room, I look around to see if there's anywhere I can hide for the remainder of the night.

"There you are," I hear my cousin Marie shout. "I've been searching everywhere for you. You were swept away by that wolf, and I nearly forgot I'm to watch over you, Sofia. You can't get that far away from me. Remember the promises we made to your father. If you do anything stupid, we'll both be locked away for who knows how long."

As if I don't know that. "And where were *you*, Marie? You promised Papa that you would shadow me."

Her face flushes, turning her cheeks scarlet. "Me? Well, I was going to shadow you, but a very hot man started dancing with me. I didn't want to be rude, so I danced with him. And then you got out of my line of sight, and I ditched the hot man to go looking for you."

"If we both just keep this to ourselves, then we'll be safe." Nothing happened anyway. My precious virginity is still intact, just as my father demands.

"I agree to that. So can we go back out there and agree to dance close enough to each other so we can see each other?"

I can't go back out there after what I've done. "Um, sure. But I need to use the facilities before I join you guys out there. My tummy's a little upset."

"Nerves, most likely. This is your first outing in twenty-two years. I should've expected this. I feel guilty too. I should've gotten between that man and you. Trouble oozed from him. What did he do to you? You can tell me. I promise not to tell a single soul a thing you say."

Longing to find out why the man made me feel the way he did, I move in close so no one else can hear. "The way he spoke — so forthright and sexual — it made me feel funny inside."

"I see." She grinned as a knowing expression made her eyes glisten. "Tingly?"

"Yes! How'd you know that?"

"It's what happens to any woman who's being hit on. That man was seducing you, Sofia." Laughing, she takes my hands, holding them close to her chest. "Tell me everything. This is exciting. You might never experience anything like that again."

"Is it that rare?"

"For you, it is. You're to be married to someone your father chooses. Someone who will help keep our Capello bloodline pure. Most likely some old geezer who has proven his ability to have children." She shudders.

I do the same, as the thought of having to marry anyone is terrifying. But having to marry some old man is the most terrifying thing I can think of. "I know you're probably right. The bloodline and how pure it stays is all Papa cares about. It means nothing to me, though. Not that I'm in charge of anything." The night isn't supposed to be this way. It's a time for celebration, and I'm not to be thinking about my future or how glum it will be. "I really don't want to talk about this, Marie. It's depressing."

"You're right. So tell me all about the man. Did he hold you close enough for you to feel a lump in his pants?"

Heat fills me as I'm reminded of the lump. "It was huge. He referred to it as his manhood too. He pretty much left nothing to my imagination."

Giggling, she pulls me in close, hugging me. "Oh, my little cousin, how scandalous this is. Your father would string us up for this. But go on, tell me more. I know there's more. A man like that, so tall, dark, and totally hot, he must have said some devilish things to you."

"He did. I don't think I can even repeat most of the things he said." Shivering with sudden chills, I step back and wrap my arms around myself. "He was hot, wasn't he?"

"Well, if you like a man with a strong jaw and chiseled features who towers above most other men, then hell yeah, he was hot!"

"And that dark hair," I add as I picture him in my mind. "So thick and wavy. The way he wears it just to the top of his collar, meaning he's more business than play. A real man. A man with power, I would bet. And the way he held my body in his strong arms..." More chills surge through my body. "Oh my God!"

"If you weren't being kept innocent for some other man, would you have given yourself to that man?" Her dark eyes hold mine, and I wonder what I would have done had he gotten me alone somewhere, the way he was obviously planning to when I broke free from him and ran away to hide.

"I'm not that kind of girl."

"You are *not* a girl anymore, Sofia. You're a woman now. A woman with a solid education. A woman with ideas of her very own. I'm not asking you if you would do it. I am asking you if you would *want* to do it."

Her question seems loaded to me. Like she might go back and report my answer to my father. "No." I laugh to hide the truth. "I'm not meant for things like that. I am special. My father has told me that from the time I was old enough to listen. I am a Capello, and I am meant to carry on the bloodline of the great Capello family. Being selfish, tending to my selfish needs, is not a thing I am allowed to do. So my answer is that I do not want to give myself to that man or any man that my father hasn't given me to."

11

With one dark brow cocked, I can see she's not buying my answer. "Spoken like a true Capello, Sofia. Smart answer. But I'm not sure I buy it."

"What's not to buy? I'm not a whore and never will be. I am a virgin who knows she can't do anything other than protect my virginity with my life. Mainly because my life is worth nothing without my virginity." Laughing, I find it's only to cover the pain of the reality of my words. Words I have heard my parents say too many times to count.

"I'm glad you're so comfortable with your fate, Sofia. I can't say that I would feel the same if our places were traded." Shuffling her feet, she looks down at them. "Of course, I gave my virginity away long ago, making myself worth nothing in the process. Had the bastard, Lenny Johnson, had any sort of backbone, he would have stood by me when my father caught us in the act. No, the shell of a man ran away, screaming that he would never touch me again. And now I'm the spinster cousin at the tender age of twenty-five who will never marry anyone of power. Best to be you, Sofia. At least you're worth something to our family."

Her story is tragic. I have been told it many times as a cautionary tale. To be worthless in a family like ours, a powerful mafia family that dates back generations, isn't something I, nor anyone, really wants.

"Why don't you go back out there and dance with some cute guy, Marie? I'm just going to use the bathroom, and then I'll go back out there. Don't worry, I won't let some man drag me deep into the crowd again. I've learned my lesson. It leaves me tingling in places that I didn't know could tingle. While it felt nice at the time, I find it's leaving me with a frustration like I've never known before."

"Ah, yes, sexual frustration. I know the old demon well. I will leave you to your business, Sofia. Be sure to come join us as soon as your tummy is feeling better."

"I will. It could take a while. Don't worry about me, I'll be right here. My stomach has never felt this upset before. Perhaps it's the alcohol since I'm not used to it. Wine, yes. Hard liquor, no."

"I'm sure that's the culprit."

Watching her leave, I feel something inside my body roiling that I haven't felt before. My feet don't take me toward a stall the way I'd planned, though. No, they take me out the door, and my eyes scan around to find the one person they wish to see.

No one ever has to know.

Chapter 3

Dante

A hand on mine sparks an electric shock that surprises me. I turn to find the little shit who ditched me earlier. "What do *you* want?" I'm not one to play childish games, and I'm not about to start now.

"To apologize."

"That's a good start." Placing my drink on the bar, I wonder what this girl really wants. "I accept your apology. As a little girl, you must not understand the ways of grown men. I fault your sheltered upbringing for that."

"I do too. And I would like to do something that I'm not supposed to do. If you're into that sort of thing." Her smile, impish, intrigues me.

"You don't expect me to fall for you shenanigans, do you?"

"I want you."

"I'm sure you do." I see nothing in her eyes that says she's ready for the likes of me. "But do you think an innocent girl like you can satisfy a man like me?"

Her expression turns into one of wonder. "I'm sorry. I don't know what you mean by that."

Unsure of why I'm giving her a chance, I take her hand then pull her along with me to my office. "Come with me, and I'll *show* you what I mean." Let's see how fast she runs when she finds out what I mean.

Amazingly enough, she doesn't pull her hand from mine, and we make it all the way to my office. She even stays as I close and lock the door. Leaning against it, I watch as her eyes move over the room.

Turning in a full circle, she takes everything in. "Is this your office? Or do you just have access to it?"

"That's none of your business." Crossing my arms over my chest, I'm not sure what I'm going to do with the little shit. "You know, women don't walk away from me. I shouldn't even be giving you my time."

"I *am* sorry." Her eyes say the same as she comes toward me. "I got scared is all. I won't walk away from you again. I swear it."

"Undress."

Stopping in her tracks, she stares at me with wide, innocent eyes. "Right here?"

"Right here. Right now. And don't make me ask again or you won't like the outcome."

"What would the outcome be?"

"Are you insane?" I can't understand this girl. But she doesn't know who I am, so I cut her a break. "Listen, don't ask stupid questions and we'll get along just fine. Keep asking them and this won't happen at all."

Chewing on her lower lip, her shy demeanor returns. "You should know that I'm a virgin with no experience at all. I've never even been kissed before."

My entire body tingles with this new information. My cock twitches uncomfortably in my pants, wanting to be set free so it can take the virginity from this girl. "What made you choose me to give your innocence to?" Why I'm asking questions when all I really want is to rip her clothes off and take her like I own her is a mystery.

There's something about taking her virginity that bothers me, though. Like it shouldn't happen this way. Not for her.

"There's something electric going on between us. I don't think I'll find another who I'm so sexually drawn to."

Of course, who am I to deny this poor girl the opportunity to be deflowered by a sex-machine like me? "Then take your clothes off and deliver yourself to me, young virgin with a hankering for my cock."

Gently, her fingers remove the thin straps of her black dress, letting it fall away from her naked breasts. Pooling around her waist, she shimmies it all the way down, leaving her in black panties and high heels. "Like this?"

"You're doing just fine." Encouraging her, I notice an odd sensation in the pit of my stomach. It's not like me to get sentimental about things — especially sex. But there's something strange going on inside my body and mind that I'm not sure I care for. "Keep going then come undress me."

Her blue eyes scan my body as she strips away the panties and steps out of her shoes, coming to me with an odd look on her pretty face. "I have never undressed anyone, other than myself. How should I go about it?"

Her novice makes me think she will take way too much time undressing me, and seeing how my cock really wants to find out what it's like inside her tight pussy, I take my clothes off myself. "Never mind."

The way she grins at me makes my heart skip a beat. Which isn't a thing my heart has ever done before. I'm not sure I like the way I'm feeling right now.

I just need to get inside her and things will go back to normal.

She steps backward until she's near the sofa. "Will this be okay?"

Moving to her with slow strides, I inspect every inch of her untouched body. My mouth waters to taste her first kiss, and I find my body quivering in a way it never has before.

Pulling her to me, I kiss her, softly, sweetly, and feel tears as they fall down her cheeks. Taking my mouth from hers, I kiss them away. "No need to cry. This won't hurt."

"It's just that I find this beautiful."

It's anything but beautiful. "You are beautiful, and I'm the luckiest man in the world to get to be with you this way." Easing her to lie on the sofa, I kiss a line down her body then give her an intimate kiss, relishing the way she moans.

"Oh my God. How does that feel so good?"

"If you think that's good, just wait." Kissing her more deeply, my tongue slips through her folds then down to the place my cock yearns to fill.

Her nails dig into my shoulders as I pump my tongue inside her. Gasping, her body tenses. "Good Lord!"

Her virgin canal begins to tighten around my tongue. Employing my finger, I let it do the work while my mouth takes her sweet, swollen pearl, licking, sucking, and nipping her into a frenzied orgasm.

Her hands move through my hair then grip it tightly, pulling hard as her body climaxes. "What's happening to me?"

With her body on fire for me, I know the time is right and move myself between her legs, pressing my erection against her tight canal that's still pulsing with the orgasm. "Here we go, baby." Forcing myself into her with one quick thrust, I nearly scream with how tight she is. "You weren't joking. You *are* a virgin."

"Was," she moans. "I'm not one anymore."

Looking down at her, I see more tears moving down her cheeks and kiss them away. "You're in the best hands you can be in, baby. It only gets better from here. Let me show you." Moving slowly, I let her body accommodate my intrusion. "You will long for more. I can promise you that."

Sliding her foot up the back of my leg, her eyes close as she moans, "I know you're right about that. This is the most amazing thing. I had no idea it could feel this good. It's almost like I'm in Heaven and not on Earth anymore."

"I can make you see God, baby." Going deeper, moving faster, I want to give her experiences she hasn't even dreamed of.

Playing with her breast, I kiss her nipple until it's erect and hard as a diamond. Sucking it as I fuck her relentlessly, I feel her body giving in to the need for release, and when she goes over the edge, gushing all over my cock, I can't hold back the orgasm that rips through my body, filling her with my hot seed.

Our ragged breaths fill the room as we both climax together. In a state of ecstasy I have never been in before, I find it impossible to pull myself out of her hot pussy that still pulsates with desire.

She clings to me, unwilling to let me go. "That was amazing. I had no idea it was like that. And I want more. You were right. I want this feeling to go on forever."

"That would be nice. But it's not going to happen like that. Like any high, it fades with time. Very little time, actually." I do agree with her, though. I want it to go on forever too.

And it could happen. At least for tonight. Moving off her, I feel the cold against my skin. "I won't be long. You just stay put."

Her blue eyes sparkle in the dim light as she watches me. "Thank you. I will never forget this."

"You sure as hell won't forget this." Laughing all the way to the bathroom, I can't help but find her innocence adorable.

Who doesn't remember losing their virginity?

It doesn't take me long to do what I need to do then return to her, the only place I care to be right now.

What I find is nothing of what I want. Her clothes are gone, and the door to my office stands wide open.

That little shit ditched me again!

Chapter 4

Sofia

A month of being kept locked in my bedroom, and still I will not admit to what I did that night. "I told you a thousand times, I was in the bathroom."

My mother's heavy bosom rises as she inhales sharply. "Your cousins have no reason to lie, Sofia. How much longer do you think your father will stand for this?"

My dear, sweet cousins ratted me out. I still can't believe they did it. Their loyalty to my father seems to know no bounds. While their loyalty to me seems to be less than none.

"Ma, I have no idea why they didn't see me in the ladies' room. I was in a stall. I have told you that a thousand times. My stomach hurt. Marie knew that too. I told her about it. She left me in the bathroom."

"There's an hour that's unaccounted for, Sofia. Your father will never accept that excuse. Your cousins have no reason to lie. They searched that bathroom, and you were not there. And then suddenly, you were there. Just tell the truth. What's the worst thing that can happen?"

Who is she kidding? My life will be as worthless as Marie's if I tell the truth about where I was and what I was doing.

"Ma, please, why can't you believe me?"

"Because it makes no sense. Your cousins said they were calling out for you. If you were there, why didn't you answer them?"

"I told you; I was sick. I couldn't say a thing. The liquor, Ma. It was the liquor. It made me drunk. The sounds were all melting together in my ears. It was terrible. I thought that was the worst of it until no one believed what I was saying. How do you think that makes me feel, Ma? I'm not a liar. I have never been a liar."

It's not easy lying right to my mother's face. But what choice do I have?

The best time of my life must be kept a secret. And what's worse is that I can never be with that man again. That wonderful man who showed me how amazing sex really is.

"There is no way that you're telling the truth, Sofia. Your cousins swear they made a thorough search of that restroom, and you were *not* there. This is unacceptable."

I cannot agree more. "Ma, I can't live this way. Please, help me leave. I don't want to be here anymore. I don't want this kind of life. I want to be happy. I can find happiness somewhere else if you just help me leave."

If I could leave this prison of a home, then maybe the man who showed me what I've been missing will take me in until I can make my own way. If I can ever find him again.

"Leave?" Her dark brows arch comically as her plump hands move to her ample waist. "Are you mad?"

She's never thought that I might want to leave our home someday?

"Ma, I have a degree now. I can make it on my own. I don't need to live here. Just help me get out of here and I won't bother you or Papa for anything. I swear, I won't."

"Sofia, do you not realize what you mean to your father?"

My jaw drops with her choice of words. "May I ask what I mean to you, Ma? I know what my father wants me for. It's you I have to wonder about. What do you get in this bargain?"

"A happy husband, and that's all any good wife should ever want."

Her archaic ways make me crazy. "Ma, this is not the stone age or the time of kings and queens. This isn't some third-world country either. This is the United States of America and the twenty-first century, for God's sakes. Haven't you heard of women's liberation? Wasn't that a thing that happened when you were a kid?"

"It happened in the sixties, and I was born in the seventies. I know all about that kind of thing. I just don't happen to agree with it. Being a wife and mother is all I've ever wanted to be. And I should think that I raised you to think the same way."

"Ma, you didn't raise me to think that way. You and Papa have kept me hidden away from the world to keep me from finding out what the world has to offer a young woman like me. And now I have a pretty good idea what else I can do, besides become the wife of some man Papa knows."

"You are not just some girl, Sofia. You were bred to become a powerful man's wife. Your father and I were matched by one of the organizations most trusted genealogists."

"Yes, I know the story well." And I hate the story. "Our blood-line is rich and full of history. Our forefathers came from Italy, and we can trace our lineage back five hundred years. Between your bloodline and Papa's, we have stayed true to our Italian ancestors, and not a drop of any other blood spoils our veins." I found the whole idea hard to even believe. "Ma, what are the chances that no one in either of your families ever had a baby of mixed heritage?"

"Believe it or not. It makes no difference to me. I know it's true. And you should too. We have taught you so much about your heritage, and we fully expect you to pass down the things we've told you. Your children deserve to know their heritage."

"Why can't I marry whoever I want?"

"You know why. You're going to become a critical piece of the plan to merge families together to make peace between our family and another. Or it might be something else entirely. Your father will decide when and what will happen with you."

"Some say I will be given to some old man who has proven his abilities to make babies. Is there any truth to that?" I hate the idea of having to have sex with some old man just to add children to our maladjusted family.

24

"That's not what I want for you. But I'm not in charge of that. If it were up to me, you'd be matched with a man closer to your age. Or at least not geriatric."

"Since neither of us has a say in who I end up being married off to, why can't I just leave?"

Going to the closed bedroom door, she pulls it open to check for any eavesdroppers and finds none. Turning back to me, she closes the door again. "Don't even speak of such a thing. You are much too valuable, Sofia. I'm sorry that you don't understand your value, but one day you will. This is not up for discussion. Your father didn't come to this decision lightly."

"And if I had been a boy instead of a girl, then what?"

"Then you would have been trained to follow in your father's footsteps. You're our only child, Sofia. God gave us only one. That makes you very special. Now, no more of this nonsense. Your father is angry with you as it is. Don't add to his anger."

"If you help me leave, I will never tell a soul what you did. I can't get out of here without someone helping me. I'll go away and never come back. I want out of this fated life you two have laid out for me. I want my own life. It's not fair that I have to marry some man I don't love."

"I had to. And it didn't kill me. You can do it too, Sofia. No reason to be so dramatic. Marriage is the same whether it begins with love or not. A husband and a wife each have duties to uphold. Love has nothing to do with the contract that is marriage."

My heart feels as if it's breaking, and all I can do is cry. "Just leave me alone. I don't want to talk to you anymore. It's obvious to me that your loyalty is not to me."

"You're right. My loyalty is to your father. It has always been that way, and it will always be that way. I'm sorry that you don't understand. One day, when you're a wife, you will understand why I stand by my husband. Do yourself a favor and get some sleep. Your emotions have taken over, and you need to get a hold of yourself. Goodnight."

I watch my mother leave my bedroom, or prison really. She doesn't care what I want. No one does.

Is there any hope for me at all?

Chapter 5

Dante

In two months, I have yet to get the shy yet spunky young woman out of my head. Why she lingers is beyond me. It's not as if there haven't been plenty of other women wanting to give me their bodies.

But I only want her.

Which pisses me off.

I've looked for her. Looked for the other ladies she was with that night. Left my men to watch for the dark-haired beauty at my nightclub on the off chance she does go back. So far, nothing. No one has seen her or anyone who was with her that night.

There's been business to contend with lately too. That alone should've kept my mind free of the young virgin. Well, she's not one any longer, thanks to me.

The assistants voice interrupts my thoughts. "Dante, your father will see you now."

Making my way into his office, I inhale the scent of expensive and illegal cigar smoke. "Father, I hope this day has been treating you well."

All I see is the back of his leather chair, a cloud of smoke hanging above it. Then he turns to face me as I take the seat on the other side of the massive, mahogany wood desk. The desk had been his father's, and the idea is that one day I will take over and the desk will belong to me.

"As well as can be expected." Opening a drawer, he pulls out a box with more cigars in it. "Join me, Son."

There are many rules in our family. If the boss is drinking, then we all drink. If he's eating, then we all eat. And if he's smoking, we all smoke. "Thank you, Father."

My father is no ordinary man, hence why I call him Father instead of something less respectful. He is the boss of all bosses in our organization. Vincent Vietti, the leader of many families, and it's his responsibility to keep everyone in line. It's no easy task, and I don't look forward to the day it'll be handed over to me.

"There has been some trouble from the Capello family."

"It must be serious if you brought me here to meet with you about it." Lighting the cigar, I inhale deeply, relishing the unique flavor a Cuban offers. Leather, cocoa, and cedar come through with the first puff. I can't help but take another, finding even more undertones; earthy tones like cherry, black pepper, and other spices that I can't quite put my finger on. "This is one fine cigar, Father. Thank you."

"Of course, it's a fine cigar." Running his hand over his face, I notice more gray hair than he had the last time I saw him. His position of power is not without its stressful downside. "Tell me what we can do to stop this incessant need for the Capello's to tread on territory that's not their own. The Maretti family is pissed about the money they're losing in their whorehouse."

"How are the Capello's taking away from whorehouses?"

"Offering the girls more money and some perks too. It's not a classy thing to do. I mean, what's wrong with the whores in their territory?"

"You want me to find out?" Puffing on the cigar, I feel the sparkling buzz the exotic tobacco is famous for and love it.

"No. I've got it figured out. If they want to take whores from other families, then I will take one of theirs." Leaning back in his dark leather chair, he sighs. "We must teach the Capello's a lesson they won't soon forget. And for that, I need you, Son."

"I'm not trying to offend you, Father. But how can taking a whore teach anyone anything?"

"It can't. No one really cares about a whore. Not *one* whore anyway. If they'd only taken one or a few, then there would be no need to step in. But the Capello's took too many from their rivals, and now I have no choice but to step in. We can't afford a battle right now."

He hasn't answered my question. My father is good at talking about an answer without really giving one. It's up to me to decipher what he wants me to do.

The wheels in my brain begin to turn and ideas pop up. "So, we take a Capello female then." Puffing on the cigar, I think about what we can do with the female we take. "We can use her as leverage against them. Make her life a living hell so they can

29

see that if they continue to step on toes they shouldn't, it will directly affect one of their own."

"This female must be special to the family too. Not just some girl they don't care about. Any ideas, Son?"

Every family has them. A few girls who are kept chaste just for special occasions. "If we take one of their special girls, then we can reign in those bastards. Wielding the girl like a weapon over their heads is the best way to get them to obey the rules of our organization."

His grin tells me he's happy with my words thus far. "And I can count on you to bring the rain when a downpour is needed?"

"Of course, you can count on me. I love doling out punishments. I think we should get a female who is worth everything to that family."

"A virgin," he mumbles as he looks up at the ceiling. "A young, beautiful virgin."

"And I will make her life a nightmare. You can trust me to teach these people a lesson they won't soon forget. Leo Capello will not continue stepping on toes once we have something that's priceless to him. He will do as he knows is right and stop this bullshit of pilfering the stock of another family's whorehouse."

"Can you trust yourself to torture a beautiful virgin, Son?"

I find his question absurd. "Father, I have no heart, if you will recall. You've taught me well. Using people to make others fall in line has been taught to me since I was a child. I can do this. You can trust me."

"I know I can. You're a good son and have proven yourself over and over again."

An idea pops into my head. "Maybe I'll even marry this virgin to further the insult to Leo Capello."

"No." Shaking his head, his dark eyes go stern. "You will not marry some lowly woman of impure blood. I had people search for the woman I married. Your mother has the purest blood and so do I. You will only marry a woman with blood equally as pure as yours."

"I didn't think about that." Foolish of me, I know. "I know it's my responsibility to keep our bloodline pure."

"To keep the bloodline pure means power. And we are nothing without power. You must always keep that in the forefront of your mind. You'll take over for me when I can no longer function as the head of this organization. And you'll have to have the right woman at your side when you do. Your children will become high ranking members of our organization, and one day it will be your eldest son who takes over for you. This is the most important thing for you to do, Dante. Never forget the importance of taking a wife who will help you lead and leave leadership when you can't lead any longer."

I know I'm important to the organization. The weight on my shoulders to do everything right is immense. But I can take the pressure and do what's right for us all. "You can count on me, Father."

"Good. I knew I could. Now, we should get to the bargaining table with Leo Capello to gain one of his best virgins. He will have no idea what we plan to do with her once she's ours."

"Once you have her, I'll take over from there. We'll bring that family under control, even if we have to mutilate the little bitch. People hate getting body parts of their loved ones sent to them."

My father's deep laughter echoes off the walls, a sinister sound. I'm reminded of just how sinister the Vietti family truly is. Placing pure blood before happiness is their utmost concern.

I know I must put the woman from the nightclub out of my mind.

There's no place for love in this family.

Chapter 6

Sofia

Eyes wide open, even though the sun burns through my open window, I'm bored to death. "When will he let me out of this prison of a bedroom?"

Two months have passed since my night of passion. Two whole months I've been kept locked away. My secret is tucked securely in; it will never get out. I can never let my father know that he's lost what has been so important to him all these years.

The door flies open, and my mother enters wearing an enormous grin. "Your wish has come true. You're getting to leave this home the way you wanted."

Jumping up, I can't believe my ears. "Are you serious?"

"I am." Grabbing me, she hugs me tightly, and I hug her back, feeling happier than I've ever felt in my entire life.

I'm going to be free!

"This is the best news ever." I'm shaking, I'm so excited. "When can I leave?" And where will I go?

I can't worry about that right now. It doesn't matter. As long as I'm free to live my life the way I want, that's all that matters.

"You will leave as soon as your father decides."

My hopes begin to cave in on themselves with mention of my father still being in charge of when I get to leave. "I see." Pulling myself out of her arms, I walk back to my bed and sit.

"You look sad." She comes to sit next to me then rests her head on my shoulder. "You're going to be given to the Vietti family. They met with your father this morning and made a bargain for you."

Immediately, I am sick to my stomach. I jump up and run to the bathroom, promptly throwing up my breakfast. Slumped on the bathroom floor, I feel as if I have already died.

Why did he give me to our family's biggest rivals?

My mother's footsteps come toward me, and she sits on the floor beside me. Concern on her face, she knows there's no way I can find any happiness in being given to our archenemy. "I know it's not at all what you expected."

"They're the worst of all families. The meanest, most cutthroat of us all. And my father hands me to them with no concern for my safety at all? I cannot understand why he would do this to me. Is it because of that night at the club?"

"Oh, no. It's not because of that at all. It's just business. Your virginity makes you worth a lot. But you know that. And you also know your father doesn't bother us with reasons why he does the things he does. So you will be taken to the Vietti's when your father says."

"They are horrible people, Ma. The stories you and others have told for years are full of torture, murder, and even worse things that that. How can you hand me over to those horrifying people? Why not just end my life now before they find a torturous way to end it?"

My stomach lurches, and I lean over the toilet, completely emptying the contents of my stomach. When I fall to the floor, my face resting on the cold tiles, my mother looks at me with concern. "When was the last time you menstruated?"

"I have no idea." And I don't care either.

She gets up and leaves me, for how long I have no idea. My life is over, and every second that passes means I'm that much closer to being given to monsters.

When she comes back, she has a package in her hands. "You need to get up and pee on this stick."

"I don't want to." I don't want to get up ever again. "I am going to lay here and die. I will never go willingly to the house of pain and anguish. That is what you all have called the Vietti estate, you know. It's not a home; it's a chamber of horrors. And my father has given me to the dungeon master himself. I have no reason to live."

"Get up or I'll have your father's men come get you up. You must do as I say."

I get up, as I don't want my father's goons anywhere near me. I pee on the stick for her then go to my bed, falling face-first on it. All hope has left me. There is nothing left for me.

"Well, this is terrible." My mother leaves the room without saying anything else.

Not that I care. I cannot find it in me to care about a damn thing. My life is over anyway. Nothing matters anymore.

My eyes move to the open window. Not only am I three-stories up, but the window is covered with iron bars to make sure no one can get in or get out. I am trapped. There is no way out for me.

When my bedroom door is thrown open, slamming against the wall behind it, I see my father's enormous form standing there. His breathing is harsh, his dark eyes ablaze, and red stains his entire face.

I have never seen him so angry. I sit up, fear coursing through my veins. "Papa?"

"You little slut! You lying whore!" Storming toward me, I prepare myself for his attack.

"Don't hit her!" My mother rushes to get between us, taking the brunt of my father's assault. The back of his hand connects with her cheek, nearly knocking her down, only she manages to stay on her feet. "She's pregnant, Leo. You can't beat her."

"Very well!" Turning around, he stomps away, shouting, "Get your filthy whore ass dressed. I'm dumping you off before they can back out of our deal." Stopping at the door, he spins around, glaring at me. "You have disappointed me more than I knew you could. You are no longer my daughter. Forget you have a father and a mother, you whore."

I gasp and immediately gulp back sobs. I can't believe it.

I'm having a baby?

Chapter 7

Dante

I am heading to the estate, as the Capello woman has been delivered. But she's not what we were told she was. And that pisses me the fuck off. We made a deal for a virgin, and Leo Capello gave us nothing of the sort. His knocked-up daughter dumped at the front door is what he gave us. Using her as leverage will be out of the question now.

But I will make her life a living hell. And when her bastard child is born, I will make sure it has a hellacious life too. She can blame her father for their putrid lives.

No one crosses the Vietti's and gets away with it. Leo will pay for what he's done.

Pregnant or not, she will feel my wrath and the wrath of my father too. If she loses her bastard baby, so be it. It's not as if I give a shit about her or the fetus she carries.

Fucking Leo Capello will pay dearly for his actions. No one goes back on any bargain made with a Vietti!

At the front entrance, I'm met by one of my father's men. "He's in his office."

Moving past him, I'm so angry I can't even speak. The amount of disrespect Leo Capello has shown my family is unforgivable. My only consolation is that I will take out all my anger on his daughter's tender flesh.

Blood will flow today!

Taking a few deep breaths, I know better than to enter my father's presence with my emotions boiling. Opening the door, I find my father sitting at his desk, his fingers steepled as he looks directly at me. "Come in, Dante."

Biting my tongue, I try to reign in my anger and take a seat. "We have been disrespected. I will take care of it, Father."

"To be saddled with a pregnant bitch is quite the show of aggression."

"I agree."

"It cannot be tolerated."

"I will handle him."

"And what about the bitch?"

With a slow nod, I take a deep breath. "I will deal with her as well. She will feel the pain for what her father has done. I don't want you to worry about a thing. I will fix this. We will get what we bargained for."

"I'll leave this up to you. Make sure he pays for what he's done to our family."

Leaving his office, I go to where the pregnant bitch is being held. Fury fills me, growing stronger with every step I take. The guard outside her door stands when he sees me.

"Leave us." I want no one coming in to save the bitch when her screams for mercy ring out.

With one swift move, I throw the door open but see no one inside. I slam the door shut behind me. I will not go searching for this bitch. "Get out here now!"

The door to the attached bathroom opens, and I can't believe who walks out. My heart pounds, my body melts, and I find myself trembling. "It's you!"

Without an ounce of hesitation, she runs to me. "It's you!"

Taking her into my arms, I suffer emotional whiplash. Fury turns into happiness in a flash, and I'm lost in her now. Her vanilla and jasmine scent hits me, and I inhale deeply. "I can't believe I found you."

Pulling back, her eyes shimmer with tears that begin flowing down her cheeks. I kiss them away, and the kisses turn to passion. Ripping each other's clothes away, we fall in a heap to the floor, our bodies wanting nothing more than to be connected again.

The moment I'm inside her, I feel like I can breathe again. Making love to her, I gaze down upon her gorgeous face. A face I have seen only in my dreams since that night. "I have searched for you."

"You wouldn't have ever found me. I was locked away." Her nails dig into my shoulders as she arches up to me. "My God,

I can't believe this is happening. I've cried myself to sleep over you every night for the last two months."

"I have thought about you every single day." Thrusting deep into her, I sigh with relief. "I will never let you go again."

"I belong to you." Tracing her finger over my lips, she looks at me with love in her eyes. "Please, never let me go."

With a soft kiss, I move with more care, as I think about the baby in her womb. "You said you were locked away. Is the baby you carry mine?"

"It is. I have not been with anyone but you. And you are my family's archenemy. A Vietti."

"And you are my family's archenemy. A Capello." I just can't believe this is really happening. "Our child will share our blood."

"Binding our families forever." Kissing my chest, she leaves a trail of fire in her wake.

The heat and passion is still fierce between us. It's like we have gone right back to that night. "You will be my wife." I won't let anyone stand in our way.

Looking at me with a smile that goes all the way to her eyes, she laughs. "If that's a proposal of marriage, then my answer is yes."

"You bet your sweet ass it's a yes." Kissing her hard, I let her know she's mine and no one will ever take her from me. My heart grows with love for her with each move we make. Undulating together, creating something beautiful.

The touch of her soft hands on my bearded cheeks bids me to look at her as she glows. Her sweet smile is all I'll ever need. "I love you. I think I have always loved you. By the way, my name is Sofia."

"What a beautiful name. Sofia Vietti sounds like the name of an angel."

"And what might I call you?"

"Dante."

"My husband, Dante Vietti." A blush covers her cheeks. "I've heard tales about you and your father."

"And they're all true too. But you have nothing to worry about."

"Because you love me?"

I never knew love before her. "I love you. I love you in ways I didn't know possible."

More tears blossom in her pretty eyes then she buries her face against my chest. "This can't be true. I was sure I would be tortured endlessly at your hands."

"Oh, I am going to torture you. You can count on that."

Looking up at me with wide eyes, fear fills her expression. "You are?"

My laughter fills the room. "With my love, silly girl!" Rolling over with her, I pull her on top of me. "You are my woman. You will be my wife very soon. My heart is yours."

Taking my hands, she pulls them to her chest. "My heart is yours too, Dante Vietti. Forever and ever. But your father is a powerful man who hates my family."

"And I am the son of that powerful man. He does hate your family. But he loves me. I don't want you to worry. I will deal with my father. You carry our blood in your veins. That carries a lot of weight with my father. Of course, he wanted me to marry someone of pure blood. But he can't have everything he wants."

"I am of pure blood." Blinking back tears, she leans over, kissing my lips softly. "I think your father will be happy with my bloodline. It goes all the way back to Italy in an unbroken line."

Knowing how much she was worth as a virgin, I can understand her father's fury. "Wow, your father must've wanted to kill you when he found out that you're not only no longer a virgin, but pregnant too."

"He did call me every bad name he could think of."

"I would bet he did. I'm just glad he didn't do anything to hurt you, physically speaking. Or I would've had to end him. Our child might not like it if I had killed its grandfather."

"My mother stopped him from beating me, otherwise, I would be black and blue right now. He was beyond furious."

"None of that matters now that I have you in my arms again. True love finds a way. I had no idea that could be true, but here it is to prove it."

Caressing my face, she looks at me with more love than I deserve. "Will you take me to see the world the way you said you would?"

43

"I will most definitely show you the world, my love. You will want for nothing."

"Can I be free? You know, not locked up in some bedroom?"

"My wife will always have freedom. And you *are* going to be my wife. Whatever I must do to ensure our happiness, I will do."

Her smile melts my heart completely. "I believe you will."

Holding her hand against my heart, I want her to feel the way it beats for her. "I never want you to worry. I will honor you as my wife and the mother of my children until the day I take my last breath. We will live our happily ever after, my love. I promise."

The End

Thank you for reading Deadly Don's Suprise Baby.

If you loved this book, then you'll love **Deadly Don's Secret Baby!**

It's a fast paced enemies to lovers Mafia romance that's bound to steam up your reading glasses.

(To get Deadly Don's Secret Baby visit: https://www.amazon.co m/dp/B0CTQYDCT1)

After declaring war on organized crime the daughter of a newly elected mayor is kidnapped and held for ransom by a New York Mafia Don. An unexpected love story then follows resulting in two pink lines and a sweet HEA ending. Read chapter one on the very next page!

Deadly Don's Secret Baby Sneak Peek

Introduction

I've been kidnapped by a Mafia grump who's given me a secret baby bump.

My father is the newly elected mayor and is at war with my captor.

Giovanni, a casino billionaire, is chiseled out of marble and simply irresistible. The perfect specimen of an alpha man with one problem - his heart is stone like the rest of him.

While locked in chains I'm seduced and thrust into seventh heaven. I never knew sinning with the enemy could feel this good.

Now with a baby growing inside me and my father refusing to negotiate, I dread that my unborn child will become the new bargaining chip.

With each passing day, the tension between us rises... As the man of stone has to choose between his criminal empire or his future heir.

(To get Deadly Don's Secret Baby visit: https://www.amazon.co m/dp/B0CTQYDCT1)

Chapter One

Giovanni

Who the fuck does this guy think he is?

My right eye twitches, my nerves already on edge, and the man's only served one damn day as mayor of the city I run. "You know, maybe he don't know how things work here in Mount Vernon."

"Maybe he needs to be told, Boss." Larry the Snake is one of my best men. If anyone can make this asshole mayor see the light, it'd be him.

"You might wanna visit this moron." Tossing back a shot of vodka, I pray it takes the edge off so my goddamn eye will stop twitching.

"Maybe you should nip this problem in the bud, Son." My father holds up a bottle of red wine as he comes into the office on the top floor of my casino. "I won this on one of the nickel slots. Just my luck, huh?"

"How do you think I should handle this?" My old man knows more about handling business than anyone I know in my organization. I trust every word that comes out of his mouth.

"Let me hear what the man has to say." He takes the remote for the television then rewinds it so he can see what we're talking about.

"Congratulations, Mayor Ricci, on your landslide victory," the reporter says with a smile. "As everyone knows, you are the high school principal of one of Mount Vernon's highest ranked schools in the New York area. Would you care to tell our viewers how you're going to leave your mark on our fair city?"

"Glad to," the smarmy old man says with a shit-eating grin. "See, I've got ideas that will change everything. We don't want to be like all the New York boroughs, full of criminal activity. That's why way back in 1894, when the citizens of Mount Vernon got to vote about becoming a New York borough or becoming an independent municipality, they chose the latter. We are our own city and want nothing like the lives of those who call New York their home. We want to be better than that. We want to know we're safe when we walk the sidewalks, drive the streets, and do business. If we're going to get back to the way things were before organized crime began creeping into our city, then we're going to have to go to war with the crime bosses who brought their illegal businesses here in the first place. I'm here to stomp out organized crime in Mount Vernon, New York, just the way I promised you all that I would when I ran for mayor."

My father pauses the television and looks at me with fire in his eyes. "You have to stop this guy or he's gonna make life pretty fucking miserable for a whole lotta people."

"Any ideas how I should go about it, Pop?"

"You see them broads standing behind him?"

Looking closer, I see what looks like the man's wife and the other is probably his daughter. "Pretty good-looking broads."

"Yeah, they are," Pop agrees. "Use the girl to get to him."

"Take his daughter hostage." With a nod, I know what I have to do. "She's gonna be some fun to play with, I can tell you that much." It's been a while since I got to torture a young beauty like her anyway. About time I had some fun in my life again.

Watching the television screen, some things begin to pop out at me. The young woman I believe to be the mayor's daughter has long, dark hair tucked neatly behind each ear. Her blue eyes sparkle brilliantly, and her ruby red lips are plump and utterly kissable. Her body is round in all the right places too.

Then there's the woman who stands next to her. A broad-shouldered woman, she stands a foot taller than her adult daughter. Thin, wispy, pale blonde hair cut short like a boys is nothing like her daughter's thick mane. There is nothing about them that's even similar.

"You notice how the mom and daughter don't look alike?" Pointing at the television screen, I find the father doesn't resemble his daughter either. "And look at the mayor. He's fat. Even with that expensive suit on, you can still tell he's fat. And his hair is gray, but you can still see a tiny bit of red hair at his temples. The girl is gorgeous, her mother is on the hideous side, and her father is about as ugly as they come."

My father shrugs. "With the way girls gussy themselves up, there's no telling what she's done to make her appear much different than she really looks."

"Well, she couldn't have made herself shorter." Laughing, I think about how I'll soon have the young woman in my clutches and then I'll find out what is fake on her and what's real. "I look forward to having her as my captive."

My father's eyes glisten as he fills a glass with the wine he won. "See, if you had yourself a real woman to call your own, you

48

wouldn't get so excited about the one you're about to kidnap. You're not getting any younger, Giovanni."

"I'm forty-two, not quite an old man as you would have me think I am. And I don't want to marry just anyone, Pop. You should know that better than anyone. I am to marry to keep our bloodline pure."

"I'm glad you've remembered that, Son. I didn't marry for love. I married for power and blood. It has served me well. My wife, your saint of a mother, has been the rock I never knew I needed. And your wife, if chosen well, will be the same for you."

"I haven't found the right woman with all the criteria I insist on. And you haven't found one for me either. In the meantime, I can play with anyone I wish. And I might wish to play with my soon-to-be hostage. Sending her back home with any dignity is not an option."

"Of course, it's not." Sipping the wine, my father makes a dreadful face. "This is no better than horse piss!"

"Why would I give away good wine at my casino?" I'm no fool. "I didn't get where I am today by giving away good things. If you want the good stuff, you have to pay for it."

"You are a financial genius." Dad leaves the glass and bottle on the table before taking out his cell phone. "We got to get this plan in motion before someone else grabs that broad. I'm calling in my brothers to help make the plan. You better get us something to eat. You know those bastards get cranky when there's no food around to keep them happy."

"A whole meal or some finger foods?" Larry asks as he puts himself in charge of the meal planning.

"It's going to be a long night of planning. So what do you think, Snake?" Dad's frown says it all. When Italians get together for pretty much any occasion, lots of food needs to be available to them and lots of wine too. The good kind.

I pause the news report, focusing on the woman who I will have in my home very soon. There's a strength that shows in her eyes. It'll be my pleasure to drain her of any and all strength she has. When she's returned to her moron of a father, he won't find the woman he saw last. He'll find a shell of a woman, almost unrecognizable as his daughter. And he will never again attempt to cross anyone in the business we're in.

For centuries politicians and law men all over the world have made vain attempts at stopping the kinds of business me and my ancestors have built. For reasons I cannot figure out, the idiots still try to end something they don't understand at all.

"Cannoli?" Larry looks at me for the answer.

"Of course, cannoli." Shaking my head, I don't know why he even had to ask. "That's like asking if you should order meatballs."

"Yeah, you're right, Boss. I'm thinking about a cheesecake too."

My mind isn't on food at the moment, so I merely nod. There's a lot to think about. The kidnapping of a family member of a public figure will mean vast amounts of publicity. And that will mean that we will have to watch our backs.

Fortunately, our organization has ties to families in New York. The mayor and the authorities won't be able to pin-point the exact family to charge with the kidnapping. Which makes things a bit easier for us.

"When the others get here, we'll get right to work." Pop settles into his favorite chair. "When will these fuckers stop trying to end something that's bigger than they can even imagine? It's like they can't wrap their tiny heads around the fact that we've always been here, and we always will be. Whether anyone likes it or not."

Yeah, we're not going anywhere!

(To get Deadly Don's Secret Baby visit: https://www.amazon.co m/dp/B0CTQYDCT1)

Printed in Great Britain
by Amazon

40345997R00037